Our Plane *Is* DOWN

a novel

by

DOUG PATON

H•I•P Books

Library and Archives Canada Cataloguing in Publication

Paton, Doug, 1980-
    Our plane is down / Doug Paton.

(New Series Canada)
ISBN 1-897039-03-4

I. Title. II. Series.

PS8581.A78396 O97 2004   jC813'.6   C2004-903758-7

General editor: Paul Kropp
Text design: Laura Brady
Illustrations redrawn by: Matt Melanson
Cover design: Robert Corrigan

2 3 4 5 6 7   11 10 09 08

Printed and bound in Canada

A small plane goes down in the bush, hours from anywhere. The radio is broken, the pilot is out cold. There's only a little water and even less food. Can Cal make it through the woods to save his sister, the pilot and himself?

CHAPTER 1

Better Than Juvie

I was not in a good mood. For starters, I was on a plane that was taking me out to the middle of nowhere for something I didn't really do. I was stuck. It didn't matter what I did or said, I couldn't get out of this one.

"Look down below," said the pilot over the headset, his voice really cheerful. "You'll see the town of Prince George."

Great, I thought. The last place that we could

land and the pilot has to rub it in by pointing out the view. I tried to ignore my fear of heights and look down.

It was my last look at the world I knew, a world of streets and cars, fast food and fun times. Now we were headed into the North – going nowhere and for no good reason.

Besides me and the pilot, there was one other person in the small plane: my sister Melissa, known to all the world as Missi. Missi was the one who started this whole trip to nowhere.

Of course, Missi had always been a problem, even when she was little. She kept getting into trouble whether she meant to or not. She stole stuff, beat kids up for lunch money and did more damage with spray paint than any kid on earth. Even worse, she got caught at everything she did. The courts finally got tired of seeing her and had run out of ways to punish her back home. So the judge decided to try something different this time.

The judge knew about some camp, way up north near Watson Lake. It was a place where kids

like Missi were sent to learn to be good. The kids lived close to nature and were taught to "appreciate" life. At least that's what they told us. The judge said it wasn't a boot camp, or like Camp Green Lake in *Holes*, but I knew it wouldn't be Disneyland.

Mom and Dad jumped at the chance to try something different. They had tried everything to turn my sister around. Missi had been grounded, fined, lectured and locked in her bedroom. She'd had love, tough love, smart love and – at the end –

no love. But nothing seemed to get through to her.

So if Missi was the kid who always got into trouble, I'm sure you're wondering why I was on the plane, too. Now that's a story in itself. Maybe my problem is that I would never let my little sister get into trouble all by herself. Maybe I was as dumb as she was.

"This sucks, Cal," said Missi to me. She was sitting right beside me, just behind the pilot. "I don't see why we have to go to this stupid camp."

"Think about it, Missi," I replied. "Even your peanut brain can remember what you did."

"Don't act like you're such a genius," she snapped. "I wasn't the only one who screwed up, and you know it."

"Yeah, I know," I sighed. I really didn't want to get into the whole thing up in the plane. We were talking over the headsets and the pilot could hear everything. Still, I couldn't just let it go. "Stealing the car wasn't my idea," I said to her. "I was just trying to make sure you didn't kill yourself."

"And you did a real good job of it, too," she shot back.

"You're just lucky you were only fifteen. Two months later and you would have been in worse trouble than this." Missi was really making me angry right now. "Do you have any idea what things might have been like? Not a camp in the woods, not community service and not just a stern warning. When you're sixteen, like now, they send you to juvie."

Missi was quiet. Maybe what had happened was starting to sink in. Maybe the kid was starting to grow up, or smarten up, or both.

"You wanna know something?" I told her. "They almost sent you to juvie anyways. Mom had to convince them that you were a good kid deep down, or you'd be doing serious time."

"You're full of it," Missi swore. "How could you know something like that?"

"I heard the lawyer talking to Mom and Dad about it," I said. "You're just lucky that a few people out there think you can be turned around."

"But not you, Cal?" she asked. It was a serious question, but I didn't give it serious thought. I just shot off my mouth the way I always do.

"No, not me. I think you've always been a jerk and now you're getting worse."

Okay, maybe that was mean, but it did shut her up. There was a downside – the silence made me nervous. Missi wasn't usually the sort of person who kept quiet. When she was mad or upset, she'd let you know it, big time.

Now the only sound in the cockpit was the loud roar of the engine. I let my mind drift off for a while, half dreaming, half sleeping.

The pilot's voice woke me up. "You kids make sure that your seat belts are buckled tight," he said. "It looks like some storm clouds up ahead. I'm going to drop down and fly beneath them, but we're carrying a lot of cargo so that may not be easy. Either way, we're in for a bumpy ride."

I leaned over the front seat and looked ahead because I was too scared to look down. The clouds in front of us were dark and threatening. I pulled my seat belt a notch tighter and got ready to be bounced around. Missi just stared out the side window as if she were bored by the whole thing.

"Isn't there some way we can fly around the storm?" I asked.

"Wish we could," the pilot replied. "But we're in a valley, so that should make it easy to go under."

It started getting bumpy before we even reached the weather. The bumps were slight at first – a jolt here, a jar there. As we got closer to the clouds, the jolts got worse. Once we got under the storm clouds, the plane wouldn't stop shaking. It was like an earthquake in the sky. We were being bounced up and down like crazy, and a couple of times we dropped so quickly it felt as though we were floating. Lightning flashed all around us. The claps of thunder were louder than anything I'd ever heard on the ground.

"How long – " I started to ask, but the rest of the words didn't get out. I threw up before they could.

Thank goodness I had the barf bag ready for it, otherwise I would have spewed all over the back of Missi's head.

Neither Missi nor the pilot saw me get sick. They were too focused on the storm.

I wiped my face and took a swig of water to try

to get rid of the taste. Then I took out some gum to cover it up with the taste of spearmint.

"I thought you said we were going under all this," I said.

"I'm trying," the pilot said, through gritted teeth, and then he added a swear word to make it serious.

Suddenly, a flash of lightning seemed to hit right in front of us. "That was a little too close for comfort," the pilot said as the thunder boomed. There was a lot of white noise in our headsets. Every time there was a flash of lightning, it got worse.

Then there was another bright flash followed quickly by a very loud clap of thunder. It was so close that I was surprised the plane wasn't hit. The pilot swore again, and his jaw got very tight. Things were bad – and then they got worse.

The engine died!

Suddenly, the only sound was rain pelting down and wind whistling by. The pilot swore again, and now I knew we were in real trouble. We were going down, fast. I can't tell you the fear in my gut and in my spine, but somehow I pushed back the urge to scream.

"Can you start the engines?"

"I'm trying, kid," he snapped back.

"What are you going to do?" Missi yelled.

"See those two big pine trees out there," he said coldly. "Unless I see some place to land, you better pray that I've got real good aim."

CHAPTER 2

Alive!

We were still caught under the storm, rain coming down like crazy, wind blowing us all over – and no power. The pilot kept pulling on the controls, trying to keep level, but it wasn't easy.

He pulled at some levers, trying to slow us down, and then aimed right between those two tall trees.

"This is crazy!" I yelled.

Missi screamed and the pilot just swore.

There was the sound of tearing metal as one of our wings hit a tree – and then we were spinning. Around and around again until something from the back smashed into my head.

When I opened my eyes, our plane – or what was left of it – was sitting on the ground. Everything was quiet, strangely quiet, even with rain still falling outside.

The quiet scared me most. If someone had been screaming, it would have been better. At least then I would have known that someone besides me was alive. Now the silence felt like the cold hand of death itself.

"Missi?" I groaned.

My sister said nothing. She was sitting in her seat beside me, her head tilted to one side as if she were asleep.

I blinked to clear my eyes.

"Missi," I cried again. I grabbed her hand and it was still warm, so I figured she must still be alive.

My vision was so blurry, I couldn't see out of my left eye. I reached up to rub it clean, and my hand came back covered in blood. I reached farther up, felt the cut on my head and tasted the blood running past my eye and into my mouth. Now I had the taste of gum and vomit mixed with blood.

I reached forward and tapped the pilot on the shoulder. "Hey, you," I said. I couldn't remember the pilot's name. It was something like Bob or Tim, something too simple and too easy to forget.

No answer.

I reach forward towards the pilot one more time. This time, instead of tapping him, I shook him a little. The pilot didn't make a sound, but I heard the sound of metal scraping against rock. Beneath me, I could feel the plane shift forward. I sat back, afraid to move.

Slowly, I went over to the window on the left side and looked out. It was so dark that I couldn't see much, but slowly my eyes got used to the dim light. When the lightning flashed, I could see that our plane had come to rest in a clearing, not far from the forest. I also saw the edge of a cliff, beside us, and running right under the plane.

My first urge was to get out of the plane as fast

as I could. It was still raining hard and I had a feeling that the ground beneath us was turning to mud. It wouldn't be long before our plane slid right off the cliff. But somehow I had to get my sister out first, and the pilot. And I had to do all that without making the plane slide forward.

There are a few really good swear words for moments like this, so I used one of them. Then I looked out the window and waited for the lightning. I did not think about the height, or falling over the cliff, or the fear I always had of that. I had to focus on what to do next.

I tried to figure how much of the plane was over the edge. I was afraid that if I moved out of my seat, the weight shift might send all of us over.

In the next flash I saw that the plane was perched with the front end over the edge of the cliff. *Okay*, I said to myself, *keep the weight in the back and we'll get out of here. Move slow and don't shake anything.*

I bent forward towards my sister and could feel the plane shift. *Whoa*, I said to myself, *bad move*. No way these guys were getting out through the front door.

Just beside me was the big door that they used for passengers and cargo. If I was going to get them out of here, that was the only way. But the space between me and the door was filled with cargo that had slid up from the back.

I reached over and felt a backpack between me and the door. I pulled it out slowly, then moved it to my knees. *Keep the weight in the back*, I told myself, *and we'll all get out of here.*

I began to grab more bags and boxes and push them to the rear. At last I could reach the door, so I grabbed the handle and pushed out. Nothing.

That's when the plane lurched forward again. I knew we were sliding towards the edge of the cliff. A gust of wind came up and made the whole plane shake. I could feel it shift and slide along the ground. *Push harder*, I told myself. I did, then kicked at the door, and slowly the metal buckled under the pressure.

When the door finally popped open, wind and rain blew in on us. The plane seemed to shake even more, and I knew we had to get out fast.

Missi wasn't very big, but she was a dead floppy

weight as I tried to move her. "C'mon, kid, wake up," I said, but she was out cold.

I got out on a step, just below where there used to be a wing. Then I grabbed her under the armpits and dragged her through the door. The rain kept pouring down and made everything slippery – my hands, Missi, the steps under my feet.

I slid Missi down to the mud below us, then went back inside for the pilot. If Missy was tough to move, this guy was worse. It took me a heck of a long time to even open the buckle on his safety harness.

At last, I did it. I dragged the pilot out the rear door, and let him slide down to the ground. Then I jumped down and dragged each of them over to some trees.

I turned back to see what I could salvage from the plane. We were going to need flares, and something to start a fire, and maybe a radio. But before I could get back up to the door, there was a horrible scraping sound.

"Oh my god!" I cried.

But there was nothing I could do. The plane

began sliding slowly forward. Its nose began to tip down, and the tail was lifting. For just a second, I grabbed at it – as if I could somehow keep the plane from falling. The plane tipped a little further, then slid and finally plunged over the edge.

This time I cursed a blue streak. Rain poured into my mouth and must have muffled the swear words that came from my lips as the plane went over.

The only sound that came back was the plane itself – falling, smashing, then exploding when it hit something down below.

CHAPTER 3

"This is just a stupid joke, right?"

I didn't sleep that night, not at all. I was too wired by everything that had happened. The mosquitoes at sunset had eaten me alive. And I was wet and chilled from the dripping rain. So I spent the night watching over Missi and the pilot, just in case they woke up. Or worse, in case they didn't.

The rain stopped before the sun came up. I'm not sure what time it was because I didn't have a

watch and the one on the pilot's wrist was broken. All I know is that when the sun finally rose, the sky was clear. The long wet night was over. We were hurt, lost, bug-bitten and alone – but we were alive.

I waited for it to get a little bit lighter out, then got up to take a look around. I looked over the edge of the cliff first. Below, the plane was a burned-out wreck. There was no way it would be good for much of anything. The plane had exploded when it hit the ground last night, but the rain had put out the flames. If anyone was going to find us, it wouldn't be because they could see the wreckage.

I turned around to look at the path the plane had taken when we crashed. It wasn't long, a hundred metres, maybe two hundred. I couldn't quite tell. About halfway down the path was one of the wings from the plane. It must have been knocked off as the pilot tried to land.

Aside from the wing, all that was left from the plane was a bag I must have pushed out while rescuing Missi and the pilot. A grumbling noise came from my stomach. *I hope that bag is full of food,* I said to myself.

No such luck. The bag only had a sweatshirt and a few magazines – *Field & Stream*, *Professional Pilot* and, strangely enough, an issue of *Cosmopolitan*. But there was a large hunting knife that might come in handy. I undid my belt and slid the knife onto it. If I was the only person able to move around, I was going to need this.

"What … what's going on?" said a voice from behind me.

Missi was up and looking very confused.

"Is this the camp?" she asked. She was rubbing her eyes and scratching at the bug bites on her wrists.

"No," I replied. "We should be so lucky. How much of last night do you remember?"

"I remember the pilot flying, and the storm," she said, "but not much after that. What happened?"

"The plane lost power, hit some trees and crashed," I told her. That was the simple story, of what had been twenty minutes of sheer hell.

"Where … what?" Missi asked, still confused.

"The plane is down there," I pointed to the edge of the cliff.

"H-how did we get out?" she asked.

"I pulled you and the pilot out," I explained, "just before the plane slid over the cliff."

A look of panic went over here face. "This isn't happening, Cal. This is just a stupid joke, right? Something that you and the pilot put together."

"No such luck, kid. We're stuck out here and there's nothing we can do about it but wait for the search party to find us."

"Yeah, like they're actually going to bother sending a search party for a couple of rejects like us."

"Speak for yourself, Missi. Besides, the pilot must have filed a flight plan. When we don't reach the camp, somebody is going to know we got in trouble. Mom and Dad will be worried sick until they find us."

"Oh, yeah, like Mom and Dad really care. Now we're going to die out here and it's all their fault."

"We're not going to die out here, you little jerk. Stop being so stupid. If our parents hadn't cared about us, you'd be in juvie right now. Me, I'd be doing community service until I'm ninety. Instead, they thought they'd try six weeks at a camp. So get the chip off your shoulder and grow up. We've got enough problems without you ragging on the old guys at home."

Missi stood there – silent, glaring at me.

"You know what? Forget it," I said. "I'm going to explore. If we're going to survive the day out here, we're going to need water and some kind of food."

"So what do you expect me to do?" Missi snapped back. "Stay here all alone while you go off and play explorer? What about bears, Cal? What am I supposed to do if a bear comes along?"

"Talk to him real nice, Missy," I said, "just like you talk to me." She snorted, but I went on. "Just stay here with the pilot so someone is with him in case he wakes up."

"Or dies, Cal. What if he dies?"

I didn't have an answer for that, so I said nothing. Instead, I looked down the path the plane had carved and started walking.

CHAPTER 4

A City Kid in the Forest

I'm a city kid. Not that Victoria is much of a city, but it's not like living in the boonies. Back home, everything we needed was there for us. The biggest hardship we faced was opening the fridge door or using the microwave. Out here, there were no fridges or microwaves. There were no supermarkets or corner stores. There was nothing but trees and rocks. How was I going to find food when I had no idea where to look for it?

On TV, it always looks so easy. You know, the shows where they put a bunch of people on some deserted island and make them survive on their own. They always seem to do okay, even if they have to eat one of those yucky crawly things. I was getting hungry enough that I might even eat a yucky crawly thing, if I could cook it. As for Missi? She wouldn't eat one for a million dollars, I was sure of it.

The path I followed smelled like airplane fuel. I walked along until I reached the broken airplane wing. It looked as if the pilot had almost made it between the two trees, but not quite.

There wasn't much I could do with the broken wing right then, but it would make a good shelter if we needed it later. Beside it there were stray bits of metal on the ground. I picked one of them up, and wobbled it in my hands. I tested it to see if it would bend and, to my surprise, it bent quite easily. *This might be handy*, I thought.

I continued down the path the plane had made, idly bending the piece of metal that I had picked up. When I reached the end of the path, at the edge of the forest, I didn't know where to go next. I also didn't want to risk getting lost. I looked up at the sky and saw that the sun was behind me. If I kept the sun behind me all the time, then I shouldn't have trouble finding my way back.

I started walking through the dense forest of trees. I hadn't gone very far when my path was blocked by a fallen log. For no good reason, I turned it over and took a look. There were all kinds of crawly things underneath it, including a few bugs that seemed to have a little extra slime. If I couldn't find anything else, I could bring a couple of those things back for us to eat. Or maybe I'd bring some back anyway, just to gross Missi out. If the guys on *Survivor* can eat them, I guess we could, too.

I wasn't sure how far I'd gone, maybe a hundred metres or so, when I saw the lake. The water was straight ahead of me in a small clearing. When I got to the edge of the water, I stopped and turned around. The sun was still behind me. I breathed a huge sigh of relief.

Finding the lake was a good thing. First, the lake

gave us a supply of fresh water. Second, a lake can be a good place to find food. I didn't know much about wilderness survival, but I knew that most of the fish you find in a lake can be eaten. It's just a matter of catching them.

I scooped up the cold water in my hands and drank like a man just out of the desert. Then, for a couple minutes, I walked along the rocky shore of the lake. There were quite a few large boulders scattered around the shore and in the water. I remembered going up to the top of Vancouver Island and finding crawfish in a lake like this. Crawfish are more or less like little lobsters, not much bigger than your middle finger. They have claws, but they're too small to hurt much. A crawfish bite is like being pinched hard by a two-year-old.

I know crawfish are a favourite food for some people, but I've never eaten one. There's something about dropping them into boiling water while they're still alive ... well, we didn't have any boiling water, anyhow.

I looked down into the lake. I could see small

fish scooting around and a few crusty-looking things than might be mussels. My dad used to order mussels when we went out to eat, so I knew they were edible. When I was younger, I got a friend of mine to eat one raw. He actually liked it and ate two more to prove it. Later on, I went back alone and tried one myself, but it was the worst thing that I had ever tasted. Still, if a person got hungry enough …

Quickly I filled up a couple water bottles from the lake, then headed back to my sister and the pilot. Just follow the sun, I told myself, but it was easier to follow the path I had trampled through the trees. I was feeling pretty good when I got back – successful, in a funny way.

"How's the pilot?" I asked.

"Still out cold," Missi replied, "and I think he's got a fever." She was sitting on a rock, all bundled up in a football jacket against the wind. "You get water?"

"Yeah," I said, handing her a water bottle so she could glug it down.

She wiped her mouth and then demanded the

next thing. "I'm freezing, Cal. Can you get a fire going or something?"

"Why me, Missi? Can't you ever do something for yourself?"

"Because … because …" and then the tears began to flow. Missi was good at crying. She'd been able to cry – on cue – ever since she was a little kid. Any time she had a problem, or something seemed a little tough, she'd just burst into tears. I'd seen enough of that to make me sick.

"Oh, cut it out, you little snot," I shouted. "Your fake crying won't cut it up here. You're going to have to get off your butt and do something."

She looked shocked, and the crying stopped in a flash. I don't think anybody had ever spoken that straight to her in her entire life.

"But, like, how?"

"Like this, Missi – you go into the woods, look around for twigs and branches, pick them up and bring them back. It's not rocket science, you know."

"But there could be bears out there," she muttered.

"Yeah, and maybe a Dairy Queen if you're real lucky – now get going."

Slowly, Missi stood up and walked off into the trees to gather wood. It might have been the first honest work she'd ever done in her life.

"Get as many sticks as you can," I yelled after her. "Small ones – nothing thicker than your arm."

I gathered up some rocks to make a firepit while Missi was grumbling and complaining in the distance. I didn't take her grumbling seriously; that's just the way Missi was. If she had to lift a finger to do anything, anything at all, she made a big production out of it.

After about fifteen minutes, I had the firepit set up. Missi had gathered together enough wood to get a fire going. So all we had to do was figure out how to get it started.

"You have your lighter?" I asked. She smoked cigarettes like a chimney, so I figured she'd have one in her jacket.

"Nope, Mom took it from me before we left. Great time for me to give up smoking, eh?"

"What about the pilot?" I asked. "Let's see if he's got one."

We searched the pilot's pockets, but we didn't find

a lighter, matches or anything that could start a fire.

"What about rubbing two sticks together?" Missi suggested. "Like they do in the movies."

It was worth a shot. I looked around and found two sticks that looked like they might work. I made a small pile of dried leaves, placed one of the sticks in the centre of it and began to rub them together.

"Just like a boy scout," Missy laughed.

"Yeah, except I was never a scout. I think I saw this in a movie once," I replied.

In the movies, of course, the guys have a blazing fire in about ten seconds. Hah! After maybe fifteen minutes, I couldn't rub any more and the sticks were barely warm. Missi took over while I took a break. She lasted about a minute.

"This is stupid!" she yelled and threw the sticks down in a huff. "We might as well be doing nothing for all we're getting done right now." Her voice was on the edge of tears – real ones – but now she was holding them back.

"Have you got any better ideas?" I asked her.

Missi just shook her head, sulking. When she got like this, it was best to just leave her alone for a while. But while we sat there, I heard a sound in the distance. It was a only buzz at first, like a large mosquito. But when the sound got louder, I looked up and saw a dot in the sky.

"Oh my god, it's a plane!" I screamed.

Missi looked towards the sky, and then jumped up on her feet.

"It's coming this way," she cried. Missy began

jumping up and down, waving her arms and screaming.

I did the same. "We're here! We're here!" we both screamed, as if anybody flying way up there could hear us.

The plane came closer, then turned right, then back toward us …

"He sees us," she screamed, "he sees – "

The pilot saw nothing. The plane turned right one more time, then flew away. In five minutes, the plane was too small to see, and it wasn't coming back.

CHAPTER 5

Fire

There are a bunch of swear words for moments like this, and I think Missi went through them all. I probably added a couple myself.

"That was just the first plane," I said to calm her down. "There will be more."

"Yeah, right," Missi groaned. "And they won't ever see us unless we find some way to signal them. We need a fire, Cal, a fire!"

"You're right, but maybe a little food would help

right now. How about some … " I said, looking around, "some of these berries."

"Do I look like a squirrel to you?"

"Sometimes," I replied, trying to make a joke.

Missi just gave me a scowl, and plunked back down beside the pilot. I walked into the woods and found a bush nearby that had raspberries, or something that looked pretty close. I came back with two big handfuls of them.

"It's these or I go get the other stuff."

"What's the other stuff?" she asked.

"I don't know what you call them," I told her, "but they're white, squirmy and live under a log."

"Eeeeeeew!" she screamed and threw an acorn at me. "You're disgusting!"

"C'mon, these berries aren't so bad," I said, stuffing some in my mouth.

"I'll starve for a while," she told me. "You said there'll be more planes, right? So maybe one of them will drop us a candy bar."

I shook my head and looked at her. My little sister, sitting on her butt, sixteen years old, but acting as if she were five. "You know what's wrong with you, Missi? You're always waiting for some candy bar to come falling out of the sky. One of these days you'll figure it out – you've got to work for what you want."

"And you know what's wrong with you, Cal?" Missi replied. "It's all the stupid lectures you give me. It's you thinking that you're so superior, when you're just as stupid and screwed up as I am."

We stared at each other for a while in silence.

Maybe we were both right, I thought. After all these years of thinking that I'm the real smart older brother, maybe I'm not. Maybe the kid was as smart as me – or I'm as stupid as she is – and it was time to face that.

"Do you think we're going to get out of here …" Missi's voice trailed off. I kind of knew what she was thinking.

"Yes, of course we will," I replied, trying to sound more confident than I felt. "They've probably got more planes looking for us right now. Mom and Dad care about us too much just to let us die out here."

"Are you sure?" Missi didn't sound convinced. To be honest, I wasn't so convinced myself.

"Of course I'm sure," I said. My stomach was jumpy as anything, but I tried to sound like I had everything under control. I wondered what those berries were doing to my gut.

We fell into silence again. The pilot still wasn't awake and his head felt hot, as if he had a fever. I was getting worried that he might die before we got rescued. It probably didn't help that he was just lying out in the open with the sun coming down on him all day.

The answer was simple. "We should build a shelter," I said to Missi. "To keep the pilot out of the sun and give us some protection at night."

"At night?" Missi asked. "There should be another plane before sunset, right?"

"Yeah, but just in case ..."

"So what are we going to do, Cal? Neither of us knows the first thing about building a shelter."

She had a point, but giving up wouldn't do us any good. I looked back along the flattened area where the plane had come in and had a brainwave.

"I've got an idea," I told my sister.

The broken wing from the plane was surprisingly

light. Missi and I had no trouble dragging it along the ground to the spot where the pilot was lying. We propped it up against a tree and dragged the pilot beneath it.

"We can use this for one side of the shelter," I said. "We should be fine if we just kind of add on to it."

"How do we do that?" asked Missi. "Pick up a couple sheets of plywood at Home Depot?"

I ignored her. After a while, I figured out that we could cut branches from the pines and weave them together into a makeshift mat. It wasn't a tight weave, but it shaded us from the sun and protected us from the wind. With luck, it might keep us dry if it started raining again.

We finished the shelter just as the sun was going down and the bugs came back in force. What we really needed was a mosquito net, but at least we had a shelter for the night. I didn't know about Missi, but I felt good about what we'd built. Now if only we could get a fire going.

I picked up a stone and tossed it up and down in my hand. There had to be some way of lighting a fire without a match, but I just couldn't think of it. Frustrated I threw the rock. It skipped down along the exposed rock of the cliff. In the dim light, I almost missed a very important detail.

"Missi! Come look at this!"

"What is it?" she asked, swatting at mosquitoes.

"Watch," I told her. I picked up another small rock and skipped it across the ground. When the rock hit the ground, it sparked just like the first one. "Did you see?" I asked her.

"See what?"

"You can be really dense sometimes, you know that?" I picked up another rock and bent close to the ground. "Here, watch." I dragged the rock against the ground and a trail of tiny sparks followed it.

"Sparks!" she said, her eyes growing bright. "Can we use them to start a fire?"

"There's only one way to find out," I replied.

I picked up another rock, a little bigger than the one I had in my hand. Missi gathered up some dead leaves and put them in the firepit.

I started hitting the rocks together. Each time

they connected, a spark flew off. After fifty tries, we still didn't have smoke, much less a fire. It didn't make any sense. Missi tried for a little bit, but got frustrated just as quickly as she had with the sticks.

Almost on a whim, I pulled out my knife and dragged the back of the blade along the rock. It sparked a lot more than it did when the two rocks hit, so I kept at it.

Fifteen minutes later we had come close twice. Each time we got a little flame and a little puff of smoke, but then it would go out. I told Missi to move to block the wind, then dragged the knife one more time. A spark jumped off and started one bit of dried bark going. I jumped down, cradled the little flame in my hands, then blew gently at it. *Give it a little wind*, I told myself, *but don't blow it out.*

Finally our little spark started to glow a bright red. Then the leaves around it caught, then a couple tiny branches, and finally – with a slight whoosh – we had a fire.

"Not bad, Cal," Missi said as the fire started to warm us up. "But I've got one question."

"Yeah," I said, our faces turning red in the light of the fire and the sunset.

"What happened to all those other rescue planes?"

CHAPTER 6

The Next Day

The sun was shining on us the next morning, but our fire had almost gone out. Quickly we threw some more dried leaves and a few dried pine branches on the fire. That brought it back.

Missi was still in a bad mood, and we both looked awful. The mosquitoes had bitten every bit of exposed skin, so now we were puffy, itchy and red. But with the fire going there was at least some hope that we'd get rescued.

The pilot was still out cold, but sometimes he would groan or mumble something. His skin didn't seem quite as hot as it had been the day before, and was kind of clammy. We decided that this was a good sign.

Frankly, I was just happy that the sun was shining and the fire would let us cook some food. Regardless of what it was we were cooking, it was better than eating berries. I won't tell you what the berries had done to me the night before.

The first thing we tried to cook was the mussels from the lake. Missi and I gathered up a bunch of them. Using a sheet of metal from the plane, we fried them over the fire. It was breakfast, sort of.

For lunch, we tried the crawfish. It took us a while to catch enough of them to make a meal.

Then we had to figure out was how to cook them. I had a hunch the best way would be to boil them, like lobsters. The problem was, we didn't have a pot. Every time we'd put a crawfish on our makeshift frying pan, the thing would crawl off. In the end, we took the piece of metal we had been using for the frying pan and bent it make a pan.

Then we boiled the water and dropped in two crawfish – that's all it would hold.

"Oh wow," said Missi as she sucked the meat out of the tail her first crawfish. "This isn't bad."

"Hey, you're right," I said. "It's sort of like lobster, except it tastes a little stronger."

And that was how we spent the day, eating crawfish, two at a time until we'd had our fill.

"Cal, I don't like to ask this again, but where are the planes? I mean, there was that one, and then nothing. Somebody must be looking for us by now."

"Yeah, well maybe the storm blew us off course," I told her. "They'd start off following the flight plan and then gradually look farther and farther off. They'll find us, sooner or later." I sounded so sure of myself, and it was just what Missi needed to hear. But the problem was, I had no idea whether it was true or not.

By sunset, there were still no planes and we were getting sick of crawfish. I started eating a few berries and Missi did the same. It's funny, when you're really hungry, anything tastes good.

We must have looked pretty awful that night. We had put on every bit of clothing we had to protect our skin from mosquitoes. Still, they found ways under a windbreaker and inside a sweatshirt hood. The itch can drive you crazy, and it sure makes it hard to sleep.

It was sometime in the middle of the night when the screaming woke me up. I sat up, afraid that some animal had attacked Missi. But the screaming wasn't from my sister. It was the pilot, sitting up, looking around wildly.

I put my arm around the guy and tried to calm him down. He was struggling a lot, but if I didn't get him calm he would only make things worse.

"Hey, man," I said to him, "calm down. We're all safe."

Finally he mellowed out enough that he could respond.

"W-where am I?" he asked.

"Somewhere in northern BC. That's the best I can tell you," I said. "What's the last thing you remember?"

The pilot thought about it. "The engine going

dead," he said. "And screaming. What happened
after that?"

"You tried to take us through two trees to knock
off the wings and slow us down, remember that?"

"No, but that must have been some pretty slick
flying."

"Yeah, except you missed one wing," I told him.
"Anyhow, the plane crashed, we got out, and then it
fell off the cliff over there," I said. "We escaped, but

that was two days ago. How long does it usually take before a rescue team is sent out?"

It took the pilot a second or two to think, but he had the answer. "They go out right away, or as soon as it's light enough to see. The team would have been sent out right after we didn't arrive at the camp," said the pilot.

"Great," Missi said, "so where are they? We had one plane, and the guy didn't see us. Since then, there's been nothing flying up there except birds."

The pilot shook his head. "The problem is, there's no telling how far off the flight path we went. And the plane will be hard to see from the air if it's at the base of a cliff. The trees are pretty dense around here, so looking for us would be like looking for a needle in a haystack. It's a good thing you've got a fire going. Somebody will see the smoke, that's for sure."

"Yeah, they'll find us."

"So what did you save from the plane?" he asked.

"Nothing much," I told him. "A backpack, this knife, a sweatshirt and some magazines." I felt embarrassed – I should have been able to get more out of it.

The pilot made a face. I could tell that he'd been hoping that I had saved something more important. "At least you managed to save the knife," he said. "Have you kids been down to see the wreckage of the plane at all?"

Missi and I both shook our heads. "We couldn't find any way down there," Missi said, "and it's all burnt up."

"Besides, we didn't want to be too far away from you in case you woke up," I added.

The truth was, checking out the plane hadn't occurred to either of us. We could see the plane from the edge of the cliff, but couldn't think of a reason to go down and look at it. Besides, I was afraid of heights. Climbing down a cliff was the last thing I wanted to risk.

"See, there's stuff in it the plane that might help us. There's an emergency kit that might have made it through a fire. Let me just get up …"

The pilot tried to stand up, but quickly collapsed back down to the ground. "Guess that right leg isn't going to work," he groaned. "Maybe one of you two could get down there in the morning."

We got the pilot, whose name turned out to be Jeff, some water. Solid food would have to wait until he felt a little better.

I managed to drift off to a miserable, restless sleep. The pilot groaned every time he turned over. It had been better, really, when he was out cold and we didn't have to think about him. Now we had to listen to his groaning through the night, and that made everything worse.

Finally, after what felt like ten or twelve hours, the sun rose and I got up. There wasn't much point in trying to sleep past sun-up, the birds got noisy and it was too bright. Besides, there was a job to be done.

I rekindled the fire and went off to the lake to gather up some crawfish. I forced Missi to collect more wood to keep the fire burning. It wasn't exactly a great morning, but sometimes you can't be picky about that kind of thing.

Jeff managed to eat a few crawfish, although he was a little wary of them at first. Missi and I also ate, always with one eye on the horizon just in case there was a plane.

But there were no planes in the sky, only the one down at the bottom of the cliff – and that was my job.

I wasn't crazy about the thought of having to climb down the cliff. I'm afraid of heights and I'm not the world's greatest athlete. But if there was something down there that could help get us rescued, then it was a chance I had to take.

Kneeling at the edge, the cliff looked pretty high. The more I stood there looking at the height, the less I wanted to climb down.

"I don't think I can do this," I told the others.

"My brother, the wimp," Missi declared.

"Okay, so let me see you risk your neck, you little …"

"Hey, take it easy," called Jeff. He was still over at the shelter since he couldn't walk. "The last thing we need is to get on each other's nerves. The first rule of survival – keep your cool. And maybe the second rule is to come up with a plan. Cal, look along the edge for any trees that come

close to the top of the cliff. Do you see any?"

I looked to my left. Nothing. All the trees stopped well before the edge of the cliff. To my right, however, there were a few that grew close the edge and that were high enough. "Yeah," I called back. "There's a few down this way."

"What kind of trees are they?" he asked.

"Um, I don't know," I was never very good with trees. You'd think a kid from BC would know something about trees and lumber, but I must have missed that week in school. "They've got flat leaves that aren't quite leaves."

"Sounds like a cedar – perfect," the pilot replied.

"Perfect?" I didn't like the sound of that.

"Yeah, it's perfect. Now come back here, and I'll tell you what you have to do."

CHAPTER 7

Down to the Plane

"You want me to do *what*?!" I was stunned. I couldn't believe what the pilot had just suggested. The crash must have really messed up his brain.

"Trust me, you'll be fine," he said. "My friends and I used to do it all the time when we were your age."

"From the top of cliffs though?" I asked.

"Yeah, we did it from the tops of houses, other

trees and even a few cliffs. Basically we'd jump from the top of whatever we could climb."

"You guys were insane," I said.

"We were just out for a good time," replied Jeff. "Besides it's the only way you're going to get down to the plane without killing yourself."

"What about getting back up?" I said. "Have you given that any thought?"

He didn't respond.

"Yeah, that's what I thought," I said, not too impressed with the plan. "What am I supposed to do, jump to the bottom and wait there till we get rescued?"

"Okay, so I hadn't completely thought that part through," the pilot replied. "But there are things in that plane that could help us get rescued faster if we got hold of them."

"You mean *if* they survived the crash and the fire?"

"Well, yeah, okay. I guess there's that, too."

I shook my head and began pacing back and forth. "We're just going to have to live without them. I'm not going to risk my neck getting down there on the slight chance that something useful survived the crash."

The pilot didn't say anything at first, he just sat there. I can't say I blame him. If I had just made a stupid suggestion like his without thinking it through, I'd be quiet, too. The problem was, I knew that part of what he was saying was right. If there was something down there that could help us get rescued, then we should find a way to get it. The problem was getting down there safely and getting back up again. It just didn't seem worth the risk.

The pilot stared up at me with a pleading look on his face. Here it comes, I thought, but he never got a chance to say anything. Missi cut in: "You guys are going to want to come see this!" Her voice didn't leave much room for argument.

"Missi, what …" I stopped dead in my tracks. Missi was standing in front of me, with a huge grin on her face. I followed her eyes out to the horizon. Way off in the distance was a thin ribbon of smoke.

I ran back to where the pilot lay. "Jeff! JEFF! There's somebody out there. There's smoke coming up over there."

Jeff shifted, winced and sat up. "Really? You're sure?"

I was too excited to be bugged by his tone. "Yes, I'm positive, there's a trail of smoke coming up. Missi spotted it."

"That's great," he said, trying hard to sit up. He seemed to be in better spirits than before. "There's no way out now – you have to go down to the plane and look for the flare gun."

"What?!" I couldn't believe he was still suggesting that. "You still want me to jump down there? There's someone out there. They'll see the smoke from our fire and be here in no time."

"Yeah, maybe," the pilot replied. "But how do they know we're not just campers or hunters? They won't know we're in trouble unless you use the flare gun to signal them?"

"We'll build a bigger fire," I said.

"Yeah, and maybe somebody will be looking for smoke signals – or maybe it gets out of control and we all burn to death."

"Then how is a flare gun going to be any better?"

"Because it shoots high into the air, it's extremely bright and it burns for a long time on the way down. Besides, even if the flare gun got burned up, you can start hiking towards the smoke. Up here on the cliff, we're just trapped."

I shook my head.

"Cal, please," Missi put her hand on my shoulder, her voice strangely polite. "I don't want to spend any more time out here. I'm tired, cold and scared. The bugs are eating me alive. If you won't do the jump down, I'll do it myself."

Missi was calling my bluff. She knew I'd never let her risk her neck by herself. The thought of her tramping through the woods, all alone, was more than I could take.

I looked at the pilot and Missi. As much as I hated it, I was the only one who could do something. Missi could stay here and take care of Jeff, and make sure that things didn't get worse. They had enough food and a supply of fresh water. I could probably find the flare, or hike to where the smoke was in a day or two. It all seemed like a no-brainer.

"All right," I said. "I'll do it."

Missi replied with that crazy grin of hers. "You know, Cal, sometimes I'm really glad that you're my brother."

"Yeah, right," I said with a shrug. "If this doesn't work, make sure you put something nice on my tombstone. Maybe something like, he kept trying to keep his sister out of trouble – right to the very end."

CHAPTER 8

Over the Edge

I stood at the edge of the cliff and looked down. It doesn't matter how high up you are when you looked over the edge of a cliff. It looks high no matter what. I couldn't believe what I was about to do – I must be as crazy as the pilot.

So I broke it down into small steps. Job number one: send the backpack down ahead of me. If I ended up going for a long walk, I'd need a few supplies. I took off the backpack and dropped it

over the edge. After a second, it hit the ground with a heavy thud.

I took a deep breath and looked down again. The closest cedar didn't quite reach the top of the cliff. There was maybe a metre or two between the top of the tree and the edge. That was a metre or two of free fall before I could grab at the branches.

Missi and I had helped Jeff over to the edge. He took a good long look at the tree, another long look at me and then down at the ground. Finally, he nodded, "You'll be fine, Cal. Don't worry. The only piece of advice that I have for you is hold on tight. Don't let go until your feet hit the ground or the cedar stops moving back and forth."

He didn't need to tell me that. I had no intention of letting go of the tree at all.

I stepped back from the edge and took a deep breath. I could feel the fear running up and down my spine, like an electric charge. I was about to do the craziest stunt ever, like one of those extreme sports shows on TV.

I exhaled, took two steps forward and leapt off the edge of the cliff.

I can't really describe what happened next. I do know this much: it was a rush. I can see why Jeff and his buddies used to do it when they were younger. It was stupid, but fun.

I'm surprised the cedar tree didn't snap when I grabbed it. Instead, it swung down under my weight, then up several times. I felt as if I were dangling from a rubber band. When the tree stopped swinging, I was left hanging only a couple of metres off the ground. That wasn't too high at all. When I dropped down, it reminded me a lot of sneaking out of my house at night to hang out with the guys.

I picked up the backpack and made sure that it wasn't damaged. It didn't have much in it, just the knife and a metal water bottle. I put the backpack on and walked over to the wreck of the plane. It looked even worse down here than it did from above.

I poked around the remains, but didn't find much that would be useful. At least nothing that wasn't broken or burned to a crisp. The radio was shot, and there wasn't any power for it. The only part of the flare gun that I found was the trigger. The emergency kit was burned beyond any use. The first-aid kit was charred and mostly melted. But there was one good thing that survived – a compass.

I looked up at Missi, who had been watching me from the top of the cliff.

"The flare gun is shot, but I've got a compass!" I called up to her.

"Okay, I'll tell Jeff," said called back.

"Can you point me in the direction of the fire?" I knew which way it should be, but I had to be sure.

"That way," yelled Missi. She pointed a finger in the direction I thought she would. I set up the compass so the needle matched up with N and tried to figure which way to go: north, northeast. Or something like that. I'd just follow the compass – north, northeast – until I could see the smoke.

"All right, I'm heading out. Next time you see me I'll bring a few Mounties with me."

The last thing I heard was Missi's laugh. Then I started into the woods.

It didn't take me long to come up with a simple

way to stay on course. The sun was mostly in the south, so all I had to do was keep the sun at my back until it moved toward sunset. Then it would be on my left shoulder, kind of. Even with the trees covering the sun, I didn't think I'd have much trouble doing that. And I could always keep checking the compass.

So I walked.

And walked.

And walked.

Jeff guessed that it would take around two days

to get to where the smoke was, providing I didn't get lost.

I kept my eyes open as I made my way through the woods. I'd need water to refill my water bottle, and I had to eat some of those red berries to keep up my energy.

This was the first time since the plane crash that I'd been able to really think. I thought about everything, all the stuff that had brought us to where we were. I wasn't especially proud of what happened, even before the plane crash.

CHAPTER 9

How It Really Began

It had all started months ago, when Missi came home driving somebody's car. She had a learner's permit, but she really shouldn't have been driving alone. So I just smiled and hopped into the car with her. Nice brother – or stupid brother, as it turned out.

"Whose car is this?" I asked.

"It's Jill's mom's," she told me. Jill was a friend of hers, a dozy girl with glasses and short hair.

"Bad guess, Missi," I told her. "Jill's mom drives

a Honda, but it says F-O-R-D here on the dash. I think that might be a clue. Now seriously, Missi, whose car is this?"

She was quiet for a moment, "John Cameron's. He left it running out in front of his place and I thought it might be fun if, well, you know."

"You stole it?!" This was a first for Missi. She did a lot of stupid stuff, but usually stopped short of grand theft auto. "Do you realize what kind of trouble you can get in for this?"

"Yeah, but we're not going to get caught," she said, flipping her blonde hair behind one ear. Then I got the big smile, the big innocent smile. "I was just going to drive it around for a while and then leave it in a parking lot across town."

"Yeah, right," I mumbled.

"John will be happy to get his car back and nobody will be the wiser, except maybe you. And you better keep your mouth shut, because now you're – what do they call it – an accessory."

Missi had been in court often enough to pick up the language. If only she'd picked up some smarts at the same time.

So there we were, doing nothing more than a joyride in a stolen car. That was bad, but soon it would get worse.

What Missi didn't know was that John Cameron was going to take his car to the garage to get his brakes fixed. So you can guess what happened when Missi stepped on the brakes to make a quick stop.

"Uh oh," said Missi.

"Uh oh what?" I was afraid to ask.

"I'm sure it's nothing," she said. "The brake pedal went down too easy and nothing happened. I'll just …"

That's when I started shouting at her, "Missi, you've got to pull over. The car doesn't have any brakes."

"Relax, will you? This happened before and then the brakes came back – I just have to pump my foot ..."

"There's a red light up ahead, you idiot, you've got to …"

And then I did something stupid. I grabbed the wheel and turned it hard right toward me. The car swerved right, jumped the curb and went through the front window of a 7-Eleven store. Fortunately no one was hurt, but we did a lot of damage to both the car and the store.

I blamed Missi for what happened; she blamed me. Looking back, I guess we were equally stupid.

Stupid was the key word. Missi was stupid to have taken the car, I was stupid to get in it, we were both stupid to keep driving it. If the courts gave out sentences for stupidity, we'd be sent away for a long time. As it was, Missi took the rap for auto theft – but she was a young offender. I got pretty much the same sentence for just being in the car with her. As I say, stupid.

And we pay for stupidity. Here I was, someplace in the northern BC woods, hungry, thirsty, tired. The sun was setting and I still had another day of hiking ahead of me. I ate a few berries, took a swig of water and curled up on some pine needles. In no time, I was out cold.

I slept until I heard the sound of something big tromping through the woods. *Grizzlies!*

CHAPTER 10

Claws the Size of My Face

I could smell them before I could see them. In the dim light of morning, the bears were little more than brown shapes in the woods – a mother and a couple of cubs, judging by their sizes. But it was the smell that got to me. They smelled like a pack of unwashed dogs, or maybe like rotting flesh.

Don't move quickly, I told myself. I tried to get my brain to work, to think what to do. There was something I read once about meeting a bear in the

woods. With one kind of bear, you're supposed to lie down and pretend you're dead. With another kind of bear, you're supposed to scream and hit it with your fist. You did one thing with black bears, one thing with grizzlies. But which was which?

Maybe they won't see me, I said to myself. But it wasn't a matter of seeing, it was the smelling that mattered. If these guys smelled bad to me, I must have smelled worse to them. So long as they stayed between me and the oncoming wind, maybe they wouldn't notice me.

So I froze. I tried not to breathe. I tried to be as still and boring as a cedar tree.

And the bears came closer. Maybe they could smell my path or the ground where I had walked. Soon they were just on the other side of the clearing. They were so close I could hear their breathing.

One of the little bears began to act frisky. Its mother reached up with one paw and gave it a whack that sent the bear cub flying. Whoo! When the mother turned in my direction, I could see its claws – they were as long as my face.

Yeah, these were grizzlies all right.

If I had a gun, I said to myself, *or a club.* But the only weapon I had was a knife in my backpack. The backpack was out in the open, a good two steps away. By the time I reached the knife, they'd be on me. And what chance did I have with a hunting knife against three grizzlies?

So I stopped breathing. I told my heart to stop beating and my lungs to stop taking in air … and I waited.

It seemed like hours before the bears went off, but it couldn't have been more than a minute to two. They weren't on a hunt for me, and I wasn't about to make friends with them. They went off into the forest and my heart began to beat again.

I was alive. It was morning and the dawn light turned everything reddish-orange. When my heart got back to normal, I realized that I was thirsty and hungry.

Jeff had said there'd be plenty of water along the way, but he was wrong about that. I'd filled my water bottle just once, and now it was empty. Even worse, those berries I'd eaten the night before weren't sitting in my stomach too well. That's all I needed – to start throwing up again.

So I started off, my mouth dry and my stomach heaving. I had a day of walking ahead of me. There were two people back at the crash site who were depending on me. I had to keep on going, no matter how lousy I felt.

And I had to keep going through bear country!

I came across water two hours later. It may have only been a small stream, but as far as I was concerned it was the best water I'd ever had. I took long, long drinks from the stream.

By noon, I figured I'd gone ten kilometres or so. Walking through the bush isn't fast and it isn't fun. I kept getting tangled up in small bushes, or tripping over stuff on the forest floor.

By afternoon, I was so starved I would have eaten my shoes. I decided to risk some of the berries again, despite what they did to my gut. There was no time to stop and fish, and nothing to go hunting small animals. For now, berries were all I had.

By sundown, I was exhausted and had been eaten alive by the bugs. If a bear had come by, I wouldn't have had any fight left. But no bears came even close, though I saw a few of them off in the distance. I sat down on a log under a pine tree, looked up at the dying light and wondered if I'd ever make it home again.

The next day began pretty much like every other day since the crash: the sun came up and I started scratching at mosquito bites. I had been dreaming about something, maybe a bear, maybe a monster. I woke up with a scream, then looked around at the forest. I shivered. Maybe I was starting to lose it, but I was sure there were shapes moving in the darkness.

Bears, I said to myself, *or worse.* This wasn't just bear country, it was Wendigo country, too. Now maybe all that is a pile of horse poop, but when you're out in the forest, hungry and scared, you can see anything.

Wake up, I told myself, but my fear was too great. They say the Wendigo calls out the name of its victim just before his death. Then it swoops down from the sky and grabs the victim by the hair. It forces him to run faster and faster. At the end,

the victim's feet burst into flames from running.

"Cal," I heard in the wind. "Cal!" Was it the Wendigo calling my name – or what? Was I about to die or was I just sick and hungry?

I could feel the hairs go up on the back of my neck.

The wind had a weird quality to it. It sounded hollow, like someone or something was moaning.... I stopped. Someone *was* moaning. There was no question now. I heard it clearly. It was low and drawn out. It seemed to ride with the wind and came from all around me. As I listened I heard another sound, it was a clunking sound. It was harder to hear over the moaning, and that made it worse.

I was terrified. Any moment I expected a Wendigo to come swooping out of the sky and grab my hair. I knew I had to get out of there, fast, but my legs were frozen to the ground. From behind me I heard the crack of a branch breaking.

"Cal!"

CHAPTER 11

A Warm Bath Is Heaven

I can't imagine what the scene must have been like. When I heard my name, I screamed to high heaven. If I hadn't been so scared, I would have run like a bat out of hell. Instead I just stood there, screaming at the top of my lungs.

I must have been a sight to see: a dirty kid screaming as though the devil himself were after him.

"Cal – that's your name, isn't it?"

Out of the woods came – not a monster – but an old lady.

"You … you're a person," I cried. I know it was stupid, and it must have sounded worse, but that's what I said.

"Last time I checked," the woman replied. "You're one of those lost kids, aren't you? I heard about you on TV."

Those must have been the sweetest words I

had ever heard. It was somebody who knew who I was. Somebody from the real world. Somebody with a TV.

The woman's name was Mrs. Rankin. As it turned out, I had almost stumbled into her yard; she and her late husband had built a cabin way out here in the woods. That's where the smoke had come from. Somehow, after stumbling through the forest for almost two days, I had made it.

Mrs. Rankin drew a hot bath for me that felt like heaven. While I was getting cleaned, she called the police to tell them she had found me. She kept asking questions through the door about where my sister and the pilot might be. "South, southwest, on a cliff!" I shouted back. Maybe that was enough.

Within an hour, a helicopter had picked up my sister and the pilot. By that evening Missi, Jeff and I were flying back home. We were on a bigger plane, this time. There wasn't a cloud in the sky the whole way back.

I think our parents were surprised that we had survived. I don't think they expected us to be as smart as we had been. As you might guess, they

were happy to see us. In fact, I've never seen them happier.

A week later we were back in front of a judge to learn what was going to happen to us. The judge decided that we had been through enough and waived any more time. "You've probably learned plenty from your time in the woods."

Maybe we had. I can see now that I'd always been putting Missi down, always tried to act like I was better than her. Maybe that was my problem. But when you're lost in the woods, eaten alive by bugs, hungry and scared – well, being stuck up just doesn't cut it. I had to work on getting smarter.

And Missi, too. I think she's figured out that her chip-on-the-shoulder thing is getting in her way. Yeah, she's got a problem with Mom and Dad, but she should stop taking it out on the world. Still, I'm not going to tell her that – I've done far too much lecturing. It's time for the kid to figure a few things out for herself. Maybe she already has.

As for me, I've talked my parents into getting me flying lessons. I don't think I'll ever feel great about flying in a storm, but I kind of like the rest of it. Jeff has put in a good word for me, and maybe there's a future in it. Besides, I've already been through a plane crash. I've dealt with hunger, bears and the wilderness. After all that, the rest of life has got to be easy.

Here are some other titles you might enjoy:

Terror 9/11 by DOUG PATON

Seventeen-year-old Jason was just picking up his sister at the World Trade Centre when the first plane hit. As the towers burst into flames, he has to struggle to save his sister, his dad and himself.

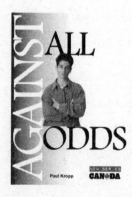

Against All Odds by PAUL KROPP

Nothing ever came easy for Jeff. He had a tough time at school and hung around with all the wrong kids in the neighborhood. But when he and his brother are drowning in a storm sewer, Jeff is the one who never gives up.

Student Narc
by PAUL KROPP

It wasn't Kevin's idea to start working with the cops. But when his best friend dies from an overdose, somebody has to do something. Kevin finally takes on a whole drug gang – and their boss – in a struggle that leaves him scarred for life.

The Kid Is Lost
by PAUL KROPP

It's a babysitter's worst nightmare: a child goes missing! Kurt has to get help and lead the search into a deadly swamp on his ATV. Will he find the lost child in time?

About the Author

Doug Paton is a young author and journalist who has interests ranging from travel to politics to comic books. Doug completed a short fantasy novel at the age of 11 and continued to write throughout high school. He has a degree in journalism from Ryerson University in Toronto. Doug's first novel was *Terror 9/11* based on the World Trade Center disaster. That book has been well received in both Canada and the United States. *Our Plane is Down* is his second novel.

For more information on the books in the New Series Canada, contact:

 High Interest Publishing – Publishers of H·I·P Books
407 Wellesley Street East • Toronto, Ontario M4X 1H5
www.hip-books.com